Maybe A Miracle

LEE PENNOCK HUNTINGTON

 Illustrated by Neil Waldman

COWARD-McCANN, INC. NEW YORK

Text copyright © 1984 by Lee Pennock Huntington
Illustrations copyright © 1984 by Neil Waldman
All rights reserved. This book, or parts thereof, may
not be reproduced in any form without permission in
writing from the publishers. Published simultaneously
in Canada by General Publishing Co. Limited, Toronto.
Designed by Nanette Stevenson
First printing / Printed in the United States of America

Library of Congress Catalog in Publication Data
Huntington, Lee Pennock.
Maybe a miracle.
Summary: Life as a minister's daughter has its good
and bad points, especially during the Depression, but
eleven-year-old Dorcas experiences the highlight of
her year when she prays for a miracle to happen for her friend.
[1. Clergymen's families—Fiction. 2. Miracles—Fiction] I. Title.
PZ7.H942May   1984   [Fic]   83-20006
ISBN 0-698-20602-9

For
KATHERINE

*To me every hour of the light and dark
 is a miracle,
Every cubic inch of space is a miracle.*
—Walt Whitman

MAYBE A MIRACLE

One

One of the ways you know if somebody is a best friend is if you never run out of things to talk about. Dorcas Bennett and Maidie Smith never ran out of things to talk about, as their mothers and their teachers very well knew. On this first warm Saturday in April, they were sitting on the front porch of Dorcas's house on Liberty Street. They had set up a wobbly-legged card table and spread out their watercolor sets and were having a delightful afternoon of painting and private conversation.

The house did not really belong to Dorcas's family, although she had lived in it for most of her almost-eleven years. It had been built in 1832, a hundred years earlier, for the minister of Saint Stephen's Church, and it had shel-

tered many rectors' families ever since. Now Dorcas lived there with her father, the Reverend Reginald Bennett, and her mother and her younger brothers, Paul and Benjie. The old house was shabby but comfortable, and Dorcas loved it.

One of the pleasantest things about the rectory was the porch with its white columns all across the front and around the side to the kitchen. It was a fine place to play, especially on rainy days. For as long as she could remember, Dorcas had watched the neighbors as they walked up and down Liberty Street on their way to and from the village green, the church down the way, or the college campus. And the porch was a fine place from which to observe the people who came to see Dr. Craigie, the town physician, whose office was in the large brick house next door.

But today Dorcas and Maidie had enough to keep them busy, what with a whole royal family they were drawing and a number of important subjects they had saved up all week to talk about.

"If you had a little sister, what would you like to name her?" Dorcas asked.

Maidie dabbled her brush in the water, frowning thoughtfully. "Geraldine is a beautiful name," she said, tilting her head and squinting at the sky. "But I like Clarissa too. My mother's cousin in Boston is named Clarissa, and she's *nice*."

Dorcas painted in a purple sleeve on the eldest princess's gown. "I like Amy and Barbara and Jenny and Katherine and Emma and Caroline and Nancy and Rachel and Rosemary and Wendy and Natalie and Susan—oh, and Isabel. All those names I like, and my parents had to call me Dorcas! Just because it's some lady in the Bible who made a lot of clothes for all her friends and my father thought that was like my mother with her sewing machine, and when she died Saint Peter brought her back to life again. *I* can't sew—I always stick the needle in my finger, and the seams are crooked."

Maidie nodded sympathetically. She had heard all this before, many times.

"You're lucky, Maidie. Madeleine is a dumb name, too, but you can shorten it to Maidie. You can't shorten Dorcas. You know what my brothers call me—Dork, Dork, legs like a stork, head like a cork, quacks like a dork!"

"Well, but you can draw and I can't," Maidie reminded her comfortingly. "What about Julia for a name?"

"I didn't used to like it," Dorcas replied. "But now I like it because I love Julia Abbot. She's my *friend*."

"I guess you can have a friend no matter how old she is," Maidie said, a little doubtfully. Julia Abbot was the wife of a young professor who lived nearby, and Dorcas often stopped to visit her on the way home from school.

"Julia understands things even if she *is* grown up," Dorcas went on. "And I never would have learned to knit if it hadn't been for her. She doesn't get impatient like Mother. When she has a baby, Julia won't give her a dumb name like Dorcas."

"Is she going to have a baby?" Maidie asked with interest.

"Of course she is. Someday. I don't know when. Lots of babies, probably. She loves babies, and she and Albert will be an awfully good mother and father."

Dorcas looked up to see her father coming up the walk with several books under his arm. "Oh, Daddy!" she called out. "You went to the library and didn't take me!"

"Well, now, Dorcas, I just stopped in there unexpectedly," her father replied in his gentle voice. "I'd been to call on old Mr. Larrabee, and the library was on the way home. I'll try to take you next time." He stood looking down at the brightly colored papers spread out around the girls. "I see you're making some pretty handsome medieval clothing for your royal family," he commented approvingly. "Next time we go to the library, you might take out a book on costume design and find some more ideas."

"I'd like that!" Dorcas responded happily. "And maybe one with pictures of what the old-fashioned ladies wore in America—Maidie really likes those best."

"We'll see," her father said, turning toward the front door. Dorcas knew he would go to his study and sit down with his new books, meaning to take but a moment to glance through them. But he would lose track of time until her mother came down from her sewing room to ask how long he'd been home.

Dorcas practiced some of the ways of blending colors she had learned from Miss Henrietta Bishop, who had been giving her lessons in drawing and painting during the past winter. Miss Henrietta knew all about how putting red with blue made purple and how yellow mixed with blue turned into green. Dorcas was explaining to Maidie the way to mix a lot of colors together to make black when Maidie whispered loudly, "Here come your brothers."

Aristotle, the collie dog, bounded up the walk wearing a pleased expression, wagging his tail. He was thoroughly wet and muddy. Paul and Benjie rounded the corner and came up the front steps, their shoes squishing with mud and their arms loaded with bamboo fishing poles, a covered pail and a basket.

"Hi!" Paul called. "You should have been fishing with us. Boy, was that water cold!" His face was lit up with a grin, and his yellow cowlick stood up from his forehead in 'an unruly crest.

"Did you catch anything?" Dorcas asked, getting up to take a look.

"Naw. Too early, I guess," Paul replied, giving his brother a shove toward the door and saying something to him under his breath. Benjie's blue eyes rolled and he giggled as he rushed into the house. Paul followed quickly and slammed the door.

"I'd like to know what's so funny," Dorcas remarked. "You'd think Benjie'd be mad they had no luck."

"Fish are horrid to clean," Maidie declared. "Good thing they didn't catch any. They'd have to cut off the heads and scrape off all the scales—ugh! Dead fish eyes— ugh! They're *awful!*"

The girls shuddered and made delicate retching noises.

The afternoon light was changing and the air growing cooler. "We'll have to go in in a minute," Dorcas murmured. "I'm almost finished—soon as I do this gold crown."

The girls were so intent on their work that they did not hear the sound of the dining-room window behind them being very carefully opened, inch by inch. Suddenly a green object hurtled through the air, landing on Maidie's painting and tipping over Dorcas's water glass.

"A frog!" Maidie shrieked, jumping to her feet and turning over her own water glass.

The long-legged creature made a flying leap over the porch railing into the barberry bushes. Dorcas sat stunned in the midst of wet and scattered papers. She heard Paul and Benjie crouched inside the window, whooping with laughter.

She sprang to her feet and shouted at them, feeling, as always when she was outraged, the hot tears spilling from her eyes. "You—you beasts!" she yelled. "Look what you've done! *Ruined* our pictures! I'll get you, I will! I'll—I'll—I'll—"

She stamped her feet in fury, while Maidie stood wide-eyed, biting her thumb.

The boys disappeared from the window, and Dorcas felt her father's hand on her shoulder. "What's all this, daughter?"

"Oh, those horrible boys! They let a frog loose and it's ruined our pictures we spent all afternoon making and I *hate* them!"

"Dorcas, Dorcas, never say you hate your brothers. They are good boys, only mischievous. I'm sorry they spoiled your pictures—that is a real disappointment after you worked so hard on them. The boys didn't mean to do that, I'm sure—they only meant to startle you."

"They did, too, they did know they'd ruin our pictures, they're just nasty and horrible and mean, mean, mean!" Dorcas cried, feeling her face grow hotter and redder with every word.

"Dorcas, hold your temper a moment and I'll go find the boys."

Mr. Bennett went into the house and was gone for a long five minutes. Dorcas and Maidie picked up the dripping pictures and laid them on the porch railing, moaning over the colors all run together and the paper shrinking in bumps and ripples.

Mr. Bennett came out again with a son held by each hand. The boys' heads were hanging, and they looked embarrassed.

"Now speak your apologies, boys," their father told them.

15

"We're sorry," Paul and Benjie mumbled. "We didn't mean to spoil your pictures."

There was an awkward silence while Dorcas and Maidie glared at the boys.

"And what else?" Mr. Bennett prompted them.

"And we're going to give you our next allowances so you can buy some more paper," Paul managed to say, while Benjie's face twisted in anguish at the thought of giving up his weekly ten cents.

"Well, girls, apology accepted?" Mr. Bennett asked.

Dorcas kept a stubborn silence for a moment. It didn't seem to her that her brothers were as sorry about the spoiled pictures as they were about giving up their allowances. At last she turned away and grunted, "Accepted." Maidie echoed her crossly.

"Not very gracious, Dorcas," her father said mildly, but he gave her an affectionate pat. "Now, boys, better see if you can find that frog and get him back to the river."

The girls, left on the porch, sat down on the swing. They pushed their toes into the floor and were rocked by the quiet rhythm of the swing and calmed by the familiar creak of its chains. Dorcas's gray cat, Aphrodite, jumped up beside them and mewed softly.

Dorcas brooded sorrowfully over the loss of her paintings. "I was going to give those pictures to Julia," she lamented. "Why do boys have to play tricks that aren't funny?"

"They don't have a proper sense of humor, that's why," Maidie stated firmly.

"Paul used to be nice," Dorcas continued. "We played together all the time. But now he just wants to do things like baseball and ship models. And Benjie was so cute when he was little, he really was. I remember, even if I was only four when he was born. Now all he wants to do is whatever Paul is doing." Dorcas wiped a last sniffle from her nose. "Boys!" she exclaimed. "Why can't I have a dear little baby sister?"

Two

"S top wiggling! I can't possibly get this dress to fit if you keep jumping around like a rabbit." Mrs. Bennett was sitting on the floor, turning up the hem of a dress she was making for Dorcas. She took the pins from a lacquered box and thrust them into the material with quick, careful movements, while Dorcas tried to stand still.

From time to time Mrs. Bennett would tell her daughter, "Turn a little bit to the left—no, not that way, to the left, you silly. Oh, not so much! Come back this way."

It was very difficult to stand perfectly straight and motionless. Dorcas would try to concentrate, staring at the pin box her father had brought from China or at the pattern in the faded rug. But then she would feel ants climbing up her spine, and a dizziness would begin to tingle in her brain, and she would just have to move her feet or her head or her shoulders. Then her mother would be cross again.

"If you want me to finish this dress for Easter, you'll have to cooperate."

Dorcas looked down at the dress, still with sleeves and hem unfinished, buttons to be sewn on, bastings to be removed. It was like many of the dresses her mother had made, of wool jersey or cotton or the rough-textured heavy natural-colored silk called pongee. The dresses were simple, loose, with rows of smocking embroidered at the neck and what her mother called "bishop sleeves." This new dress was of dark-blue linen with red and white smocking.

"I don't know why I can't wear Cousin Trudy's dress for Easter," Dorcas complained.

Cousin Trudy, who was thirteen, lived in New York, and once or twice a year a parcel of her outgrown clothes would be sent for Dorcas. Out of the rustling tissue paper would come the loveliest dresses, wine-colored velvet or yellow satin or rose-patterned watered silk, and, one time, a glorious flowered hat. Dorcas could never understand why her mother was not pleased with these splendid clothes, why she hardly ever allowed Dorcas to wear them.

"I've explained to you before," her mother replied impatiently. "This is 1932. The whole country has been suffering from a Depression for three years. Banks failed, factories closed. Fathers out of work, families hungry. People are having a dreadfully hard time. Your Uncle Harry seems to be one of the few still doing well, so he can afford fancy clothes for Trudy. But it wouldn't be right for *you* to go around looking rich." Mrs. Bennett's voice

19

softened as she sat back on her heels and looked at Dorcas. "Cousin Trudy's dress just wouldn't be suitable, dear. You don't need to wear velvet and lace to church. This dress is quite stylish enough, simple and appropriate."

Dorcas did not say aloud, "But it's not as pretty!" She did ask, as politely as possible, "Maybe this year I could wear Trudy's hat?" She knew her mother had packed it away in the attic. Sometimes, when no one else was home, Dorcas got it out and, standing amidst the old trunks and storage boxes, she tried it on before the big cracked mirror in the corner. It was the most beautiful hat in the world, with a satin brim and a wreath of tiny roses and bright-scarlet cherries around the crown. Dorcas felt that in such a hat she might, even with freckles and skinny braids, be mistaken for a princess.

"I'm sorry, dearie. That hat is not the thing for the rector's daughter. You would look grander than any other child in the parish, and that wouldn't be right. Your straw bonnet will do nicely, and I've bought a new navy-blue ribbon for it."

Dorcas sighed heavily. That straw hat was four years old—why, she'd been barely seven when it was new. It was perfectly plain, with babyish streamers down the back. Even Maidie had a hat with daisies on it. Now that Dorcas was almost eleven, surely she ought to have a more grown-up hat. But there was no use arguing once her mother made her mouth into a firm line like that.

Mrs. Bennett looked at the row of pins in the hem. "Walk over to the window and let me see if it's even all around. S-l-o-w-l-y, so I can tell if it's the right length. For pity's sake, Dorcas, don't lift up your arm! How can I—oh, well, there, I do think it will do. Come here and let me unpin the back so you can take it off."

"Hooray!" Dorcas cried, wriggling out of the dress and

back into her pleated skirt and old green sweater. She was almost out of the room when her mother spoke.

"I don't feel you're very grateful, Dorcas."

"I'm sorry!" Dorcas exclaimed, rushing back to give her mother a hug. "Thank you for making me the dress, Mother." But she couldn't add, "I like it very much."

Racing down the stairs, Dorcas went to the kitchen, feeling in need of a glass of milk and five or six oatmeal cookies. She had settled herself at the kitchen table, with glass and plate and the new book of Russian fairy tales Uncle Harry had sent, when Paul came in.

"Get your own cookies!" Dorcas cried as he snitched one from her plate.

"We're supposed to share cheerfully, aren't we?" Paul asked innocently, giving her pigtails a tug. "Daddy's going to plant the garden," he added.

"When?"

"Right now. Look out the back door."

Dorcas got up, taking the cooky plate with her. She could see beyond the iris border to the garden plot that had been plowed the day before by old Mr. Twitchell, the church sexton. Aristotle was sniffing at the freshly turned soil. Her father was standing with a ball of twine beside a wheelbarrow full of stakes. Cramming the rest of the cookies into her pocket, Dorcas ran out to join her father. Paul helped himself to the cooky jar and followed along, munching noisily.

"Can I help, Daddy?" Dorcas called out.

" '*May* I help.' Yes, indeed you may," her father answered. "Take half these stakes over to the far side of the garden and we'll measure out the rows. Thank the Lord for this fine weather. My grandfather always told me, when the maple leaves are big as a squirrel's ear, it's time to plant the peas and lettuce."

21

Dorcas looked over to the big maples behind Dr. Craigie's house. Sure enough, the new little leaves were just the size of a squirrel's ear.

Benjie came chugging around the house, making noises like a truck. He squatted beside Dorcas and picked up a long wriggling worm. He dangled it beside her ear, but she would not give him the satisfaction of squealing. Their father gave them a lecture on the usefulness of earthworms, which kept the soil turned over so that plant roots could find their way downward and grow strong.

In the trench her father had dug, Dorcas carefully dropped peas in along the wire fence that the vines would climb. She covered each pale-green wrinkled pea with an inch or two of soil, patting it down firmly. "Isn't it funny," she remarked, "that seeds have to go down in the dark before they can come up to the light?"

"They need the dark to grow roots and start their stems and leaves underground," her father replied. "It is a miracle how a tiny seed can hold everything it needs to become a mature plant. God works in mysterious ways His wonders to perform."

Dorcas recognized the line from one of her mother's favorite hymns.

"Chickens grow in the dark, too, inside the egg," Benjie spoke up from where he was enthusiastically tramping down soil over a row of early beans.

"And animals and people inside their mothers," Paul added.

"And ideas inside heads," said their father. "Books. Poems. Sermons. All growing in the dark of our skulls. Some like good seeds and some not." He fell silent, and Dorcas thought he must be planning a sermon about seeds, good ones and the other kind.

The children worked happily with their father for over

an hour, laying out rows and pouring out seeds from the packets with their bright pictures of perfect orange carrots, perfect crimson radishes, perfect emerald-green peas. At last their father said, "That's all for today. We got a great deal done, working together. In a day or two we'll put in the potatoes and the squash. Now I have to go in and work on my sermon."

Dorcas put her hoe away in the barn and washed her hands at the kitchen sink. Her knees were brown with dirt as well, but she decided they could wait for the bath after supper. There would be just time now for skating down the hill for a short visit with Albert and Julia.

Dorcas liked to skate fast downhill, but on the way to the Abbots' house she often stopped for a moment at a little park in the next block. It was a quiet place with old pine trees and a few benches. By an ivy-covered wall stood a statue of a Civil War soldier, a young man striding forward with his head high, rifle in hand, pack on his back. Around the base of the statue were carved the names of the men of Gordontown, the "heroes who sacrificed for the cause of the Union."

When Dorcas and her brothers were smaller, they used to climb up by the statue and pretend to be soldiers and heroes. She remembered that one time when her father had seen them playing there with sticks for rifles, he had said something—she couldn't quite recall the words— something like "You don't have to be a soldier to be a hero." Nowadays, if she sat on one of the benches to tighten her skates or catch her breath, she studied the names and thought about the men who had gone to war to keep the states united and to set the slaves free. Some of the names she knew about—Jonathan Smith was Maidie's great-grandfather, Phineas Morris was the great-uncle of her classmate Richard Morris, and Hiram Baxter was an ancestor of another boy in her class, Grover Baxter. Some of those men had died in battle, some had come home injured. They were all dead now, but their families, those who still lived here, remembered them almost seventy years later.

Today Dorcas did not stop at the park, only waved at the statue and kept on rolling downhill.

Albert and Julia Abbot lived in a small white house with dormer windows that always looked to Dorcas like sleepy eyes in a square face—the front door was the mouth opened in surprise. A neat picket fence surrounded the lawn and the little garden, and there was a gate that squeaked the way Aphrodite did when she wanted a saucer of milk.

Albert, an astronomy instructor at the college, had twinkling eyes behind big spectacles, and he always had a joke for Dorcas. Julia was small and pretty, with dark hair. Her smile was generous, but Dorcas had noticed that sometimes in church, when she was not aware of anyone looking, Julia's face was very sad and she seemed to keep her head bowed in prayer longer than other people in the congregation.

Julia welcomed Dorcas at the door. "Come in, dear. You're just in time for a cup of cocoa."

Dorcas took off her skates and followed Julia through the cheerful book-lined living room into the tiny kitchen.

Julia soon had a pot of cocoa on the table beside two of her best cups and saucers. "My grandmother was famous for painting china," Julia said. "She did the roses on these cups and saucers—oh, forty years ago." Dorcas studied the flowery garlands closely, marveling at the careful brushwork. "She gave them to my mother, and my mother gave them to me. I wish . . ." But Julia did not say

24

what she wished. She turned her head and began stirring her cocoa busily. "Wouldn't you like a marshmallow in yours, Dorcas?"

"Oh, yes, I love marshmallows!" Dorcas exclaimed. But she was not distracted from wondering what Julia had not finished saying. She knew it was rude to ask prying questions, especially of grown-ups. But Julia was her friend and might not be angry. Dorcas decided to ask her directly.

"When I grow up, my mother is going to give me the silver teaspoons her mother gave her," Dorcas said. "Do you want a little girl so you can give her your teacups someday?"

Julia looked startled, then sorrowful. "Yes, Dorcas, I would very much like to have a little girl. Or a little boy. I'd like to have lots of children."

"But . . ." Dorcas did not know how to continue. She bit her fingernail for a moment, then blurted out, "But why don't you have a baby, then?"

Julia did not answer right away. "You see . . . I was going to have a baby. And then I lost it."

"Lost it?" Dorcas was bewildered. "You lost your baby? Where?"

"Oh, Dorcas, I mean—I mean it died before it was ready to come into the world."

Dorcas sat speechless. She did not quite understand what had happened, but she felt shock and sorrow. At last she said the only thing she could think of to be of comfort. "But, Julia—you could have another baby."

"It doesn't seem possible, I'm afraid. Dr. Craigie doesn't think it will ever happen. Sometimes that's the way it is."

"Oh, dear, Julia, I wish you could. I'll put that in my

prayers. And if you do, I'll come and help you. I can change diapers—I've practiced on Mrs. Crockett's baby. And I know a lot of songs to make babies go to sleep."

Julia got up and gave Dorcas a kiss on the top of her head. "Bless you," she said. "I can't think of a better helper than you'd be. Maybe—maybe there could be a miracle . . ."

Dorcas skated home so deep in thought she hardly noticed the cracks in the sidewalk. How could Julia lose a baby? Why couldn't she have another? How did miracles happen? Albert and Julia needed a baby. God ought to let them have one. Was there anything a person could do to help make a miracle? She would have to ask her father.

Three

Miss Endicott, pale and plump, sat at her desk at the front of the schoolroom while her pupils bent over their spelling books, studying for the weekly test. The room was very hot. Radiators hissed and steamed quietly, and every once in a while a heating pipe banged and gurgled. Outside, a spring rain fell softly and the trees at the edge of the schoolyard seemed to grow greener each hour.

Dorcas had written out all the columns of words very quickly. She never had any trouble with spelling and was sure she would get them all correctly on the test. If only she could do arithmetic as easily! Maidie always got poor marks in spelling, but she could solve arithmetic problems with what seemed to Dorcas magical ease.

There was no use going over the words again—*medication, handkerchief, demonstrate, conversation, equinox,* and all the others in this week's list of forty new ones she already knew by heart. Maybe it would be safe to do a little drawing. Miss Endicott had let her piercing gaze wander over the class just a moment before and had gone back to her own book; it might be a while before she looked up again. Dorcas carefully slid out a fresh piece of paper from under her spelling book. She propped the book up on two erasers to make a little protection for her drawing paper and began quietly penciling in a scene of a castle with banners flying from the towers.

She was making designs of lions and fleur-de-lis on the pennants when she felt a nudge on her shoulder. She did not look back to the desk behind her—she knew it was Grover Baxter passing on a note from Maidie. At the beginning of the year, Maidie had sat behind Dorcas, and note-passing had gone on constantly. One day Maidie sent nineteen notes to Dorcas and Dorcas sent sixteen to Maidie. But Miss Endicott had put a stop to that, moving Maidie to the last seat in the row and putting Grover behind Dorcas. Horrible Grover, with his hair growing down to his big thick black eyebrows, and his big rubber boots smelling of manure. He never spoke a word to Dorcas if he could help it, but he could be relied on to pass on notes.

Dorcas's hand slid to the rear of her seat, and she grasped the tightly folded note from Grover's hand. She put it in her lap and waited a moment to be sure Miss Endicott had not noticed. Sliding the note on the open bookshelf of her desk, Dorcas opened it slowly and read Maidie's message written in sprawling letters:

Can you come over this afternoon.
XXXXXOOOOO
Maidie

P.S. Philipp Hawkins saw miss Endicots
bloomers when she leened over to erasse
the blakbord.

Dorcas stifled a giggle and risked looking back to the last seat in the row, where Maidie sat looking entirely innocent. Dorcas made a silent Yes with her mouth and Maidie grinned back.

Just as everyone was moving restlessly, shuffling papers and closing books more vigorously than necessary, Miss Endicott made an announcement. "We'll have the spelling test now, class. Put away your books and practice sheets. Rosie and Philip, pass out the paper. I want you to use pen and ink and remember that neatness counts. You'll have twenty minutes for the test, and when it is over I have a surprise to tell you about."

"Surprise? Surprise!" Everyone began asking questions, but Miss Endicott firmly demanded silence, and soon there was only the scratching of steel pens as Miss Endicott read out the words. Dorcas could hear Grover breathing heavily behind her, and saw Priscilla Goddard in the seat ahead trying to lift her pen from her inkwell with great care but making awful blots on her paper anyway.

When all the papers had been collected, the children sat up straight with hands folded on desks, looking expectantly at Miss Endicott. She patted her untidy nest of hair and smiled at her pupils.

"Now, since it's so wet we can't have recess outdoors today, everyone stand up for exercises."

There was a great clatter and some quiet groans as the class rose to its feet.

"Up with your hands. S-t-r-e-tch! Breathe deeply. Now stre-e-e-e-e-e-etch again . . ." Dorcas saw what everyone else saw as Miss Endicott raised her arms high: white ruffles edging the bottom of a pair of pink bloomers.

"Now—bend to the right, then to the left. Deep breathing again. Repeat . . ."

All the boys breathed so deeply they sounded like locomotives, and Dorcas tried hard to keep from laughing.

"Very good. Sit down, everyone, and take out your copies of the *Odyssey*."

Dorcas loved the story of the Greek hero Ulysses which they had been reading for several weeks. Yesterday they had come to the last chapter, telling of Ulysses' return to his island home after twenty years of wars and wandering.

When they had all taken out their books, Miss Endicott put on her toothy smile and announced, "The surprise is that we are going to put on a little play. Since we've finished reading the *Odyssey,* we'll act out some of the scenes of Ulysses' adventures. After we've rehearsed them sufficiently, we'll give a performance at the school assembly and invite your parents to come."

Everyone made pleased noises as Miss Endicott continued. "We'll do the part where Ulysses sails safely past the sirens. And the part where he escapes from the cave of the one-eyed giant. Then the scene where the enchantress Circe turns Ulysses' sailors into swine. And last, Ulysses' homecoming to his faithful wife, Penelope."

Dorcas was filled with happy anticipation. There was nothing more exciting than being in a play—learning the lines and rehearsing until all the parts came together, putting on costumes and makeup, and finally the electrifying moment of the performance and then the audience all applauding. She had been in several school plays, and at home she had written and put on five or six dramas in which she and Maidie were usually the heroines and Paul and Benjie were persuaded to be knights or dragons. But this would be a real performance, on the stage of the school auditorium, with a large cast and everyone in the John Quincy Adams School watching.

Miss Endicott passed out papers in which she had written scenes with speeches and directions for each character. Excitement ran through the class, and everyone waited anxiously for Miss Endicott to announce who was to take which part. Dorcas squeezed her eyes shut and prayed silently, Please, please, let me be Penelope!

"Richard, you are to be Ulysses." Dorcas was happy. Richard Morris was the boy she liked best in all the class, though she hoped it was a secret from all but Maidie. He had light crinkly hair and bright rosy cheeks. He was not a sissy, but his shirt was nearly always clean and his knickers neatly buckled. Richard was shy and never said more than "Hello" to Dorcas or the other girls. If he smiled at her once in a great while, Dorcas felt her face redden and her heart beat pleasantly fast.

"Philip, you're the tallest boy in the class, so you are to be the giant Polyphemus. Maidie is Circe, Rosie and Martha and Winifred are sirens, Grover is Ulysses' son Telemachus . . ." Miss Endicott went on with her list and came to the end.

Dorcas was alarmed. Miss Endicott had not mentioned the part of Penelope, nor had she assigned any role to Dorcas. Didn't Miss Endicott want her to be in the play?

That couldn't be true! Dorcas swallowed hard and raised her hand. "Please, Miss Endicott, what about Penelope?"

"My goodness, of course. I overlooked that, I'm afraid—it's right here. Penelope. Yes. Dorcas—you are to be Penelope."

A wave of happiness made Dorcas want to dance. She was so pleased that she didn't even mind that Grover, who was too tongue-tied to be a good actor, was going to play the role of Telemachus, the son of Penelope and Ulysses. Maybe I'll be an actress instead of an artist, she thought jubilantly.

In the confusion of moving Miss Endicott's desk and of the actors in the first scene finding their places in the front of the classroom, Dorcas felt a poke from Grover. She reached back for the note from Maidie. It said: "What if Ulyses has to KISS Pennelopy when he gets home HA-HAHA."

Dorcas's stomach churned with a mixture of joy and nervousness. She took a scrap of paper and wrote in very small letters: "I don't care."

Four

The Saturday morning before Easter, Dorcas and her mother had taken over the kitchen to prepare the Easter eggs. First they boiled them until they were hard, then they dyed them in basins of water colored by onion-skins, beets, spinach and blue ink. Then Dorcas spent a long time with her paints and brushes, decorating the eggs with flowers, whirls and squiggles, and funny faces.

Easter morning was cold and damp, but Mrs. Bennett got up early and hid the eggs among the iris leaves, under the lilac and forsythia bushes, and even in the birdhouse and the clothespin bag on the laundry line. Dorcas thought she herself was a little old for an Easter-egg hunt, but after breakfast she went out with her brothers, each carrying a straw basket lined with shredded green tissue paper.

Paul found the first egg, then Benjie crowed proudly as he discovered two more. Dorcas decided not to look very hard, because Benjie was so eager to be the one who found the most. And he did, with ten eggs in his basket, eight in Paul's, and six in her own. The eggs were all taken in and arranged in a cut-glass bowl on the white linen tablecloth on the dining-room table, where they looked very fine indeed.

Sometime after their father had left, Mrs. Bennett and the children walked to church, taking their seats in the front pew. Dorcas would much rather have been seated in the back, where she could see everyone and not have everyone staring at her, but Mrs. Bennett always said their father wanted his own family in the front pew where he could see them, and they were not to "turn around and gawp." So Dorcas in her new dress and old straw hat sat quietly next to her mother, who was looking very pretty in her good blue coat and last year's hat freshly trimmed with a small bunch of cloth daisies and a tiny veil. The boys in their Sunday suits were sitting up straight, their hair slicked back neatly and their fingernails cleaner than usual.

The scent of lilies on the altar filled the church, and as the organist began the Easter hymn the choir came in loudly singing "Alleluia." Dorcas was always proud to see her father in his vestments at the end of the processional. When he stood in the pulpit and said, "Let us pray," Dorcas bowed her head and silently asked blessing on everyone in her family, her friends, especially Maidie, and Julia. "And please," she added fervently, as she had been doing regularly now, "please let Julia have a baby."

35

It was a long service, with special music by the organist and the choir. Richard was one of the choirboys, and Dorcas thought he looked like one of the angels in a print of a painting by the Italian artist Botticelli that hung in her father's study. Dr. Craigie sang a solo in a deep voice that vibrated when he held a long note. At the end, some rays of sunlight beamed through the stained-glass windows while her father held up his hand to say, "The Lord bless us and keep us. The Lord make His face to shine upon us, and be gracious unto us. The Lord lift up His countenance upon us, and give us peace, both now and evermore. Amen."

Back home, Dr. Craigie and Miss Larrabee, Dorcas's Sunday-school teacher, joined them for the Easter dinner. Dorcas had groaned when she was told Miss Larrabee was coming. "Now, you must be kind to her," Mrs. Bennett warned. "You know she can hardly ever get away from that bad-tempered invalid father of hers who doesn't want anyone else to take care of him." Today Miss Larrabee looked happy, with two bright-pink spots on her cheeks.

They sat down at the table, which Dorcas had helped to set with the best china and silver. Their father said a rather long grace, with special thanks for the celebration of Easter, and for the food they were about to be served, with reminders that those in need should not be forgotten. Dorcas was particularly thankful for this dinner of all her favorite foods—roast chicken, potatoes and gravy, green peas and butterscotch pie.

"That was a fine Easter service," Dr. Craigie declared, unfolding his napkin while their father carved the chicken. "Fine sermon too, Reginald. Yes, I'll take a drumstick, if you please, and a slice or two of the white meat."

Miss Larrabee cooed like a pigeon when she tasted the

stuffing. Hairpins were falling out of her frizzled gray hair, and whenever she swung around in her seat to talk her long green beads clanked against her plate. She ate very daintily, with her little finger crooked.

Dr. Craigie gave Mrs. Bennett many compliments. "You're a superb cook, madam," he said, bowing in her direction and sawing away at his drumstick. "It's a treat for a lone widower like myself to share a family meal like this."

"You must come oftener, Doctor," Mrs. Bennett told him.

"Like to, indeed, but I'm kept pretty busy these days. Lot of influenza around, and after this hard winter people don't seem able to resist it." He shook his head and looked worried. "Too many people out of work, not eating properly. Hard on the old ones and the little ones especially. No proper heat in their houses, no decent clothing."

"We all know you help by not sending bills to your patients who'd have a hard time paying," Mrs. Bennett said.

"Ah, well, yes." Dr. Craigie looked embarrassed. "But some of 'em are too proud, and if they can't pay they just don't come. They just stay away and get sicker. That's the worst of this Depression for a doctor."

"It's gone on for so long," Miss Larrabee said, her long face drooping. "I think of all the talented little ones who ought to be getting piano lessons. I'd be glad to teach them without charge, but the parents won't allow it."

Dorcas felt guilty, eating such good food and wearing a new dress. Aphrodite slithered around among the legs under the table, and Dorcas reached down to stroke the soft fur. She saw her parents' serious faces and felt helpless at the thought of all the sadness in the world.

"I'm afraid it is a very bad time," her father was saying. "People in bread lines in the city. People selling apples on the street corners. Farmers leaving their farms to go West where they hope things will be better. A very bad time. I'm afraid President Hoover simply cannot deal with it. Perhaps a new President in this year's election will make some changes for the good."

"I think you'd make a good President, Daddy," Paul offered.

"Thank you, son," Mr. Bennett replied. "But, like Calvin Coolidge, I do not choose to run."

Everyone smiled at that, and from then on the conversation was more cheerful. Dorcas was glad, because her mother always said that cheerful conversation at the dinner table was the best thing for digestion, and Dorcas did not want indigestion after all she'd eaten at this Easter feast.

When Dr. Craigie asked her how she was doing at school, Dorcas told him about the play and he listened attentively, laughing when she described how cross Miss Endicott was when people forgot their lines or didn't come on stage when they were supposed to. "So you're to be Penelope," he exclaimed. "I'm sure you will make a splendid queen, my dear. Perhaps I can slip into the back of the auditorium and see this performance. Then when you are a famous movie star I can say I saw you in one of your first roles."

Miss Larrabee giggled, and Dorcas blushed. She knew that Dr. Craigie was only teasing, but he meant to be kind. Maybe when her brothers grew up their teasing would be like that, the sort that made you feel better instead of worse.

After Dr. Craigie left, Miss Larrabee insisted on staying

to help with the dishes. Dorcas sneaked upstairs to her room and changed into her everyday clothes. Out by the barn, the boys were trying to play quietly so as not to disturb their father, who was taking his Sunday-afternoon nap.

Dorcas took the script of the play from her desk and looked over her lines. She had memorized them easily by the second rehearsal, but she liked seeing them in print.

"No, no, I cannot marry anyone until I finish weaving this tapestry," Dorcas declaimed, keeping her voice low so that no one outside her room would hear her. She tried saying it in several different ways, changing the intonation and becoming more and more theatrical. She was quite pleased with her last version.

Now if only Richard and Grover would practice being more dramatic. Richard always forgot to raise his voice, and Grover kept standing like a fencepost, with his eyes on the floor. Girls were ever so much better at acting, Dorcas reflected, and wondered why. It would be too bad if the play were spoiled because the boys did badly.

With a sigh she flopped onto her bed and stared at the ceiling. Aphrodite strolled into the room and leaped up beside her, curling contentedly into a ball. She must have been given some chicken scraps in the kitchen, Dorcas thought. Aphrodite purred like a little teakettle for a moment, then closed her eyes.

"You're having a catnap, Aphrodite," Dorcas told her. "Maybe I will, too."

It was nice to have holidays and visitors and celebrations. But it was nice to be private, too, in your own room with nobody else there except a sleeping pussycat.

Five

At *three o'clock* there was a knock on the bedroom door. Dorcas was instantly awake. "The sun is shining," her father said. "Want to go for a little walk with me?"

"Oh, yes!" Dorcas called back. "Let me get my sweater." She loved going for walks with her father. He could give her his full attention and talk to her without interruption. He would point out an ancient oak tree, or a house with an old-fashioned door, or an oriole's nest. She felt grown-up, quiet and contented in his company.

Today they walked out past the college buildings to the woods at the edge of town. The air was warmer, the sun peeking in and out of the high clouds.

"Look there, Dorcas," her father told her, pointing with his cane. She saw a big patch of violets just coming into bloom at a clearing in a stand of birch trees.

"Aren't they beautiful! That means spring has really come. Shall I pick some to take home?"

"I think you might. But why not do it on the way back, so you won't have to carry them? We'll walk on a little farther now."

Beyond the woods a dirt road stretched out between fields, some newly green, others fresh-plowed into chocolate brown. Red-winged blackbirds called from the elm trees lining the road.

Dorcas felt this was a good time to bring up a subject which had been troubling her. "Daddy, do you have to pray for a miracle, or does it just happen?"

Her father slowed his walk to a thoughtful pace. "That's a good question," he responded. Dorcas was grateful that he did not say, "Go look it up," as he often did because he wanted the children to get used to consulting the dictionary on the dining-room sideboard and the encyclopedia in the glass-doored bookcase in the hall. "I can't give you a quick answer. People have puzzled over that problem for a long time."

They walked on, going uphill now where old stone walls marked fields and pastures. "It does seem that a miracle can be in answer to somebody's asking for it," her father continued. "A prayer by the person who needs it, or by someone who cares very much for that person. That is what happens in the Bible stories about Jesus' healing of the blind men and cripples, and bringing the dead to life. Yet all kinds of miracles are given to us every day without our asking. Just look at this grass coming up green after being dead all winter. We don't think to pray for it, but

we're given it every spring. That's a miracle, too, isn't it?"

"Yes," Dorcas agreed. "But lots of times people pray for things, like their grandmother getting well or finding a hundred dollars so they can buy food and clothes for their children, and it doesn't happen. Maidie has been praying to be a good speller for two years and she's worse than ever." She didn't tell her father about her own prayers for Julia. Somehow she was a little shy about that.

"That is a great mystery, my dear, why prayers are sometimes answered and sometimes seem not to be," her father replied. "I believe that we often ask for the wrong things, or perhaps at the wrong time. Our prayers may be answered in a way we don't expect, or at a different time, which may be far better for us."

Dorcas thought about this for a moment. She didn't much like the idea of anyone, even God, deciding what was best for her. Her parents often said they were doing just that for their daughter, and Dorcas quite often did not agree, at least at the time.

"But if you *know* what is best for someone else—not yourself—and if you prayed hard enough, there could be a miracle?"

Mr. Bennett looked down at Dorcas's earnest upturned face and seemed about to ask a question. But he did not, only said gently, "Why, of course it could. But don't be too disappointed if it doesn't, if something quite different comes along. The situation could change and you might not need that miracle after all."

Dorcas was not entirely satisfied with this advice. However, she determined to go on with her prayers for Julia, feeling that since they were not just for herself, God ought to pay more attention.

By now they had passed two or three farms and had come to the top of the little hill. Here a house and a barn had been built close to the road. "That's where Grover Baxter lives," Dorcas pointed out to her father, who had been walking along with one hand behind his back, deep in thought.

"So it is. I know Mr. and Mrs. Baxter, though they don't come to church. Grover is in your class, I believe."

"Yes, he's the oldest boy. He has some brothers in the lower grades. Grover sits right behind me, and, Daddy, he lots of times smells of manure."

"That's a good farm smell," her father said. "It must mean Grover is helping his father in the barn. Farming's hard work, you know, and Grover may not have time in the morning to tidy up before he comes to school."

Dorcas felt a little ashamed of herself for having been so critical. Her father always saw the other side of the picture when she complained.

The farm did not look very prosperous. The barn roof was sagging and the red paint almost gone. There was no paint at all on the house, with its rickety porch and bare front yard. Dorcas saw a woman on the porch, but when they came nearer she got up and went into the house, the broken screen door creaking as it closed behind her.

Now a man came limping around the corner of the barn. He wore overalls and a battered felt hat. "That's Mr. Baxter," her father said. "I believe I'll have a word with him."

Dorcas tagged behind her father to a rusty gate in the barbed-wire fence. "Good day, Mr. Baxter," her father called out.

Mr. Baxter came toward them slowly. "How do," he said shortly.

"Happy Easter to you and your family," Mr. Bennett said in his kindly voice.

Mr. Baxter looked away toward a spot where a high old

black automobile sat tipping over near the porch. "Same to you, Reverend."

"This is my daughter, Dorcas. She tells me you have a son in her class."

Dorcas murmured how-do-you-do, and Mr. Baxter nodded his head.

"How are things going with you, sir?" Mr. Bennett asked.

"Not so good. It was a rough winter, spring's late and wet. Plow's broke. Can't get at the planting. My leg's given out."

"Have you been to see Dr. Craigie about it?"

Mr. Baxter turned away. "I'll get into town some day."

"Better not neglect it, my friend," Mr. Baxter said. "And Mrs. Baxter?"

"Poorly. Lot to worry about. She won't go to the doctor."

Mr. Bennett shook his head. "The two of you must take care of yourselves, you know. You have a big family to think of."

"Yes, Reverend, I know. Five young ones. So far." He looked at Dorcas and said nothing more.

Dorcas felt uncomfortable, her hair whipping in the breeze and her eyes not knowing where to look.

"You are welcome to come see me anytime, if you wish," Mr. Bennett told him.

"I know that, Reverend. Thankee."

"Well, we'll be getting on home now. Come along, Dorcas." Her father took her hand and they turned back toward town.

Dorcas felt as if there were many pairs of eyes staring at her as they went past the barn and down the road.

The day did not seem so pleasant now. The sun was not really warm, the breeze was growing sharp. Dorcas had to stop to unlace her shoe and take out a pebble that had given her heel a bruise.

She spoke in a low voice. "They're awfully poor, aren't they?"

"I'm afraid so," her father replied, shaking his head. "Sometimes people work very hard but have bad luck and just can't get ahead."

"It doesn't seem fair," Dorcas said indignantly.

"No, it doesn't. It's especially sad for parents when, no matter how they try, they can't do what they want to do for their children."

Dorcas was silent, thinking how fortunate she was. It was silly to be sorry for herself because she didn't have a new Easter hat. She resolved to be friendlier to Grover.

Her father did not have much to say on the homeward way. They were coming down Liberty Street before Dorcas realized they had walked right past the patch of violets and she had not remembered to pick an Easter bouquet.

Six

Miss Endicott held a finger to her lips and spoke in a fierce whisper. "You simply must keep quiet, class. The audience can hear you out front when you make such a racket."

Actually, the children were not being noisy. Crowded backstage in Assembly Hall, they were too nervous to do much talking. Dorcas, in her Penelope costume with yards of white sheeting draped into a Grecian dress by her mother, felt chilly enough to shiver. She was certain that her hair, tied with a gold ribbon in what her mother assured her was a Grecian style, would tumble down before she ever got on stage. Maidie, looking pale and wearing a gown very like Dorcas's, also made by Mrs. Bennett, was reciting her lines under her breath.

Dorcas stole a look at Richard. He was dressed in a short tunic with a band around his head and ribbons laced up his bare legs. His lips were pressed so tightly together Dorcas wondered if he would ever be able to get a word out, or give her the kiss he was supposed to plant on her cheek in the last scene. When they had rehearsed this part, Richard had never actually kissed her, but just brushed his face against hers. Dorcas hoped that this was because he was shy, not because he didn't like her.

There was a subdued sound of voices beyond the stage curtain as Assembly Hall filled up with classmates and parents. There would be more mothers than fathers in the audience, but Dorcas had been told both her parents would be there, and of course her brothers were present with their classmates in second and fourth grades. She wasn't sure if she was glad to have her family there or wished that none of them had come. It had been bad enough having Paul and Benjie teasing her about her "white nightgown" costume and being "married" to Richard and "mother" to Grover Baxter. Now they would perhaps be seeing Richard kiss her, and they'd never let her forget that.

Miss Endicott looked around in sudden agitation. "Where *is* Grover?" she hissed, waving the play script in her right hand. They heard the music teacher begin to play "America the Beautiful" below the stage.

"Where is Grover?" Miss Endicott repeated, her eyes searching frantically from one face to another among her pupils. The fifth grade, huddled together in the semidark, turned their heads and tried to discover Grover in their midst. They suddenly realized they had not seen him all morning.

"Are you sure he's not here?" demanded Miss Endicott. "Not just hiding or playing tricks?"

"No, Miss Endicott," Philip piped up bravely. "I don't think he ever came today."

"Oh, for pity's sake!" Miss Endicott burst out, quite loudly. She couldn't have been heard by the audience just then, for they were all busy reciting the Pledge of Allegiance. "Whatever shall we do? Let me think . . ."

"Maybe Philip could be Telemachus," Dorcas suggested timidly.

Philip glared at her. "How can I be Telemachus if I'm already the giant Polyphemus?" Philip muttered. He was dressed in a sort of fur tunic made from his father's old coonskin coat, and he held a knobby stick that was supposed to be the giant's club. "I'm too big to be Telemachus, anyway."

Miss Endicott gripped Philip's shoulder. "You'll have to be Telemachus, Philip. You're only in that early scene as the giant, so you can just change into one of the sailor's outfits and take that part in the last scene. Here, take this page and study the lines. I'll tell you when to go on and where to stand. You can do it, Philip." She stared at Philip so grimly that he did not dare to argue. Swallowing hard, he took the script Miss Endicott pressed into his hand and began reading the lines in silent panic.

Now they could hear the principal, Mr. Higgins, making announcements. "And, finally, we come to the major event of today's program, a presentation of scenes from the *Odyssey* by Miss Endicott's Grade Five. Priscilla Goddard will name the cast and announce the scenes."

Priscilla, standing next to Dorcas, seemed paralyzed.

"Get out there!" Miss Endicott whispered crossly, giving Priscilla a shove.

Priscilla went out like a sleepwalker to the center of the stage as the curtain went up. It seemed at least five minutes before her voice, high and trembling, could be heard reading off the names of the cast. When she got to Telemachus, son of Ulysses, she stumbled over Grover Baxter's name, paused, looked around wildly, and went on. The audience applauded loudly, and Priscilla scurried back to her waiting classmates and burst into tears.

"None of that, Priscilla," Miss Endicott said sternly. "You did very well. Now, class, I expect you to give a splendid performance. Everyone do his darnedest."

The children had to smile. Miss Endicott had never used such a slang expression before, and they felt somehow bolder and determined not to disappoint her. They would do their darnedest.

The first scene, with Ulysses talking to his sailors about the Trojan War and coming to the island of Circe, went better than they'd expected. Everyone in the audience laughed when Maidie as the enchantress Circe turned the sailors into swine. When the curtain went down, to enthusiastic applause, the players rushed backstage flushed with triumph. From then on, the scenes went without too many lines being forgotten or stage fright making anyone altogether speechless.

At last the final scene arrived, and Dorcas, taking her place on the stage beside her loom (made of several bed slats and twine), pretended to be weaving a tapestry. The boys who played the parts of her suitors went through the motions of feasting and wrestling. When they asked Penelope when she would marry one of them, she told them in a throbbing voice, "No, no, I cannot marry anyone until I finish this tapestry."

Then little Mickey Murphy, in a rough brown sweater and furry ears and tail, as Ulysses' faithful old dog, barked loudly in recognition of his long-absent master. Mickey lost his tail as he rolled over and died. There was a lot of laughter from the audience at this, which Dorcas thought very inappropriate, but she was concentrating on the words she had to say at the appearance of Ulysses: "Oh, my beloved husband! I cannot believe my eyes! Is it really you, returned after twenty years?"

Ulysses came on, disguised as an old man, and challenged the suitors to a contest with his own mighty bow and arrow that had hung on the palace wall all during his absence. When he proved that only he was strong enough to draw the bow, everyone at last recognized Ulysses, who promptly set about slaying all the suitors.

Then Richard was beside Dorcas, and she felt what was very like a kiss on her right cheek. Her hand flew up to the spot and she turned bright pink while Richard spoke his lines: "I greet you, faithful Penelope, after long wanderings. And is this my son Telemachus?"

Philip stood wordless, having completely forgotten his newly learned lines. There was a dreadful silence. Suddenly Dorcas heard her own voice saying words that were not in the script: "Yes, Ulysses, this is your son Telemachus. He has been a good boy."

Philip suddenly found his voice. "Yes, Father," he squeaked. "I am your son. I have taken care of my mother while you were—while you—while you were absent in heroic battles."

The rest of the scene—with Penelope explaining how she had told all the suitors she would marry only when she finished the tapestry which she then unraveled each night, and Ulysses telling of his years of adventurous voyaging to get back to his island home, and his promise never again to leave his wife and son—all went amazingly fast. Dorcas could not believe that it was over so swiftly, with what sounded like thunderous clapping when the curtain fell. Everyone went on stage again for a bow, and then the curtain went down for the last time.

Miss Endicott, looking pink and pleased, was surrounded by the girls, who were actually hugging her and
talking all at once.

"Oh, wasn't Richard good when he killed the suitors!"

"Did you see Maidie kick Harold when he wouldn't
turn into a swine fast enough?"

"Ooooh, I forgot half my lines!"

"Miss Endicott, was I all right?"

Miss Endicott positively beamed. "You all did ex-
tremely well. I am proud of you."

When they got back to their own classroom, they found
their mothers and fathers there, full of congratulations,
and a punch bowl of lemonade, and plates piled with
cookies. For once, Miss Endicott said nothing about low-
ering voices.

Dorcas gave her mother a hug and remembered to
thank her for making the costumes. Her father handed
Dorcas a small bouquet of violets.

"Leading ladies are supposed to get flowers from their
admirers," he told her. "You were charming, Penelope. I
am sure Homer would be delighted to know his great epic
is still being read and acted today."

That night when she went to bed, Dorcas realized with
an unexpected sense of loss that she no longer had to
worry about her performance in the play. It was all over.
But, oh, it had been wonderful. Especially when Richard
kissed her, really kissed her. She smiled in the dark and felt
again the place on her cheek where his lips had been for an
instant. It was such a warm and pleasant memory that she
knew she wouldn't even mind her brothers' silly teasing.
It had been a beautiful day, splendid, as Miss Endicott
would say.

Just before she fell asleep, a question flashed into her

confusion of happy thoughts: Where was Grover Baxter? Why hadn't he been at school, today of all days? But she could not keep her mind on that mystery, and in a moment she was dreaming of giants and white dresses and kisses and looms and barking dogs and violets.

Seven

Sometimes Miss Henrietta Bishop's arthritis was so painful she could not stand at her easel and paint. But today she had telephoned Mrs. Bennett to say that she was feeling "spry" and Dorcas could come for her Saturday art lesson.

Dorcas put her watercolors and brushes into her school bag and slowly walked the three blocks to Miss Henrietta's cottage. There were doorway lilacs in bloom at nearly every house, and rows of iris with purple, white and lavender blooms bordering the lawns. It was a cool, sunny morning, and Dorcas thought regretfully of Maidie and her other friends who would be playing outdoors. But she did like her art lesson, and her teacher.

Miss Henrietta had taught drawing at the college for almost a lifetime. Now she was retired, but, except for the arthritis days, she still took great pleasure in teaching and had a few private pupils like Dorcas.

Huge old lilac bushes nearly filled up the tiny yard beyond Miss Henrietta's gate. Dorcas rang the bell, but knew that Miss Henrietta, who was quite deaf, had probably not heard it. She walked into the little parlor, dark and cluttered with old-fashioned furniture, and then to the back room Miss Henrietta had made into her studio. Here there was good north light from two large windows, and a delicious smell of paint and turpentine.

Miss Henrietta turned from her easel, where she had been studying a painting of a blue vase filled with lilacs. The canvas was shiny with wet paint. Dorcas saw the still life set up on a table near the easel and noticed that the flowers were drooping.

"Good morning, Dorcas. I've been trying to paint these lilacs for three days, but it hasn't gone as I'd wish." Miss Henrietta sighed and pointed to the canvas. "As you see, the blue of the vase is too harsh, the highlights are not brilliant enough. But I shall continue to strive."

She stood with her head on one side, squinting through her pinch-nose spectacles at the canvas. She was thin and stooped, with gray hair piled atop her head in a style that had been fashionable in her girlhood. Under a gray smock she wore a high-necked blouse and a long black skirt.

"Get a glass of water, Dorcas, and then I'll start you on your assignment. Today I want you to do a watercolor study of three iris in this white vase. You may go out to the garden and pick three in the colors you prefer."

Soon Dorcas was seated at the drawing table, dipping her brushes in water, mixing paints, trying to capture the

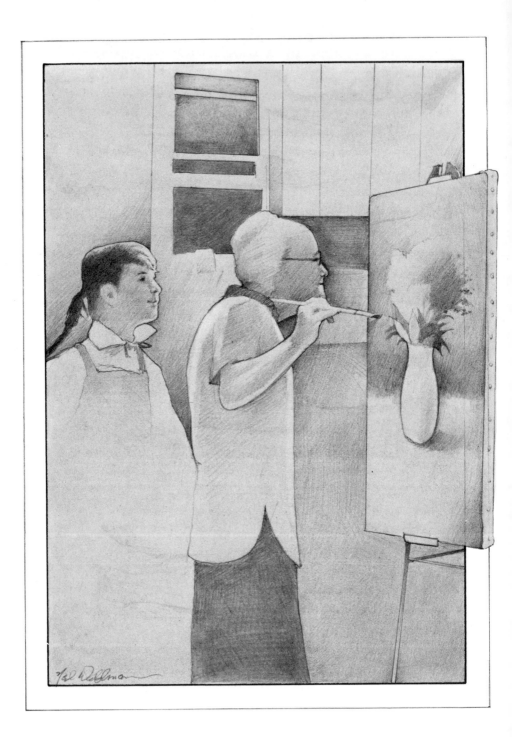

shape and colors of the iris blossoms before her. It was not easy. One of the iris blooms was purple and white, one was pale yellow, and a third a soft blue-violet shade, and there were stiff green leaves as well. Miss Henrietta hovered over her, speaking of perspective and color ranges and advising a darker tone here or a rounder curve there. Dorcas concentrated, not aware of time passing. She was surprised to hear the sound of the grandfather clock in the parlor striking twelve.

"It's noon!" Dorcas exclaimed. "I didn't realize the hours had gone by so fast."

"That happens when you are absorbed in your work," Miss Henrietta observed. Dorcas saw that Miss Henrietta was white-faced and that she was leaning on her cane. She must be awfully tired, Dorcas thought, maybe in pain.

"I did work hard at it," Dorcas said, looking at her morning's achievement—five different versions of the three iris in a white vase. She picked up the last one. "I think this one is the best," she said. "But it's still not the way I really wanted it to look. You could have done it so much better, Miss Henrietta."

"Well, my dear, I have been painting for sixty years longer than you have. That ought to make a difference. But, you know, even after all this time, I often have just your feeling of not being satisfied with what I've done. Like these lilacs which I'm going to have to start over entirely. The thing is not to be discouraged, but to keep striving." Miss Henrietta took her spectacles off and then put them back on her nose. "I was brought up on that fine saying of the philosopher Ralph Waldo Emerson: 'Not failure but low aim is crime.' One can't help failing now and then, but it's no solution to give up and settle for something easier. One simply must keep one's aim high."

57

Dorcas didn't mind Miss Henrietta's lecturing. What she said was usually pretty sensible, and quite like what Dorcas heard at home all the time anyway. What she admired was Miss Henrietta's determination not to turn into a complaining invalid but to insist on keeping busy and independent. Dorcas hoped that when she was an old lady she would be like that.

On the way home, Dorcas stopped at Julia and Albert's house. Albert was working in the garden, weeding a row of lettuce. "Hello, Dorcas," he called. "Julia's in the kitchen, serving up lunch, I hope. Go on in."

Dorcas found Julia stirring a pot of soup that smelled appetizing.

"You look hungry." Julia smiled. "Would you like a bowl of soup?"

"No, thank you—I mean, yes, I would, but I'm expected home. I just stopped to give you a picture I made this morning." Dorcas took out the three best paintings from her satchel and found a place on the kitchen table between the bread and butter plates to spread them out. "You can choose the one you want."

"Why, Dorcas, thank you. What a nice idea. But, oh, my, they are all so pretty, how can I choose?"

Dorcas knew which one really was the best, but she didn't point it out. It really should go to her own parents. But if Julia selected it, Dorcas was going to let her have it.

Julia took several minutes to make up her mind. At last she took up one and declared, "This, I guess, is the one I'll take." It was the picture Dorcas considered second best. "I do like the way the petals curl, and the color of the leaves. Albert will like it, too, I'm sure."

Julia went to the door with Dorcas and gave her a hug. "I'm lucky to have this picture of the iris to remind me of spring even when winter comes," she said. "Your parents are lucky to have such an artist for a daughter."

On the porch step, Dorcas turned and said softly, "I'm not forgetting about praying for a miracle for you, Julia."

Dorcas went home, to find that the boys had already eaten lunch and gone off to a baseball game. Her parents still lingered at the table, eating a second helping of rhubarb pudding. They admired the paintings, and Dorcas enjoyed a little time with them without the usual interruptions from her brothers.

Leaving the dining room to go to his study, her father turned to ask Dorcas, "By the way, has Grover Baxter been in class this week?"

"Grover? No, he hasn't, Daddy. He hasn't been back to school since the day before the play. I don't know what's the matter with him. Measles, maybe. A lot of people have measles this week. I think Grover's little brothers have been absent, too."

Her father looked grave, but said nothing further.

Mrs. Bennett told Dorcas to wash the dishes and added that Maidie had telephoned to ask if Dorcas could come over that afternoon and stay for a picnic supper.

"Hooray!" Dorcas cried. "It's going to be a nice day all day." And she went cheerfully to fill the dishpan in the kitchen sink.

Eight

That night Dorcas decided to sleep out on the sleeping porch. It was a large screened space over the kitchen, with several old metal beds furnished with horsehair mattresses from Grandfather Bennett's farmhouse. On hot summer nights the whole family slept there. Sometimes Mr. Bennett slept there even in winter. "It clears my head," he explained. "Nothing like it after a day in the study." Now on this pleasant May evening Dorcas thought she would like the feeling of openness to air and the night sky.

She was very fond of her own bedroom, with its flowered wallpaper her mother had pasted up herself, the old cherrywood bed with carved pineapples on its posts, the bookcase with all her books from *Mother Goose* to *The Oxford Book of Verse,* the dollhouse that had belonged to Aunt Margaret, the old cushion by the window where Aphrodite often curled up for a nap. But sometimes it was good to feel free of everything except a plain bed in a place where the breeze blew fresh all night long.

When she had snuggled into bed under a faded quilt, Dorcas lay listening to the night sounds—a sleepy bird in a nest in the maple tree, a car wheezing uphill toward the college campus, Dr. Craigie's old Buick coming into his driveway after a late house call. A few minutes later she heard the doctor singing "Indian Love Call" at his piano, but then he closed his living-room window and turned out the light. He usually went to bed early because he never knew when he might be called out in the middle of the night.

Dorcas thought about the picnic at Maidie's house, about Julia and Albert, Miss Henrietta and her lilacs, and about her own paintings. Perhaps she could try again to do some iris and get the colors better. She would look tomorrow in their own iris border for some she could put into a vase and paint, taking as long as she needed to get them right. She would go down early tomorrow before breakfast, before the sun had made the dew disappear, and pick the best ones she could find. She would set her "inside alarm clock" to wake up early so that she could get it done before everyone was up and getting ready for church. Dorcas sighed contentedly and curled into a ball under the quilt, letting the blackness spread under her eyes and into her head until everything was dark and quiet and she slept.

Dorcas woke with a start. It was not yet quite daylight, still very early. Had her inner alarm clock wakened her too soon? No, it was something else that had disturbed her sleep.

A sound.

What was it?

She listened, but there was only deep quiet everywhere.

No, there *was* something—a thin crying note. Where did it come from?

Wide-awake now and a little frightened, Dorcas got out of bed and looked across the garden. The sound seemed to be coming from Dr. Craigie's house.

There it was again. At first she thought it might be a kitten. But it was a different note, somehow, not like an animal.

The sound continued, a little louder. With a sudden leap of her heart, Dorcas realized that it was a baby crying.

But how could that be?

The crying could not have come from inside Dr. Craigie's house. It must be outside, but where? She could see through the maple leaves the light that always burned by the side door to Dr. Craigie's office, but there was nothing to be seen in the circle of its shining.

Dorcas shivered in the cool dawn air and pulled the quilt around her. The crying had stopped. She listened intently for a moment, wondering if she had been dreaming.

Then she heard it again, and was quite sure.

It was without doubt a baby, and it seemed to be just about at Dr. Craigie's front doorstep, where all was dark. She strained her eyes, but saw nothing but shadows.

How could a baby have gotten there?

Dorcas gasped aloud. Somebody must have left the baby on Dr. Craigie's doorstep. On purpose.

She would have to tell her parents.

Dorcas turned to go into the hallway, but just then she

saw a light go on at the doctor's front door. Dr. Craigie, in a nightshirt and with his hair all on end, stood looking down at a basket at his feet. Dorcas saw him lean over and pick it up. She thought she could see a tiny red face in a mound of white blankets.

Dr. Craigie went into the house and closed the door. The light over his front door went out.

Then lights went on upstairs and down in the doctor's house, and Dorcas had a glimpse of old Mrs. Reilly, the housekeeper, coming into the kitchen and bending over the stove. What was happening over there? Maybe the baby was sick. Dr. Craigie would know what to do for a baby, but why would anyone bring it to the doctor and leave it like that on a doorstep instead of coming inside?

Dorcas, shocked and puzzled and wide-awake, tiptoed into the hallway and stood outside her parents' bedroom. She longed to burst in and wake them with this astonishing news, but she had always been told that her father must not be awakened at unreasonable hours, especially on Sunday, when he needed his sleep before rising to go to church for the seven-thirty early service.

She thought about going into Paul's room and sharing the news with him. But Paul was always hard to rouse, and their voices might disturb their parents.

Dorcas leaned over the bannister to see the clock in the downstairs hallway. It was only ten minutes of five. It would be at least an hour before her parents woke. Dorcas did not see how she could contain her story so long, but there was nothing for it but to wait.

She stopped in her bedroom to pull on her bathrobe, then crept down the back stairs to the kitchen. From there she looked over to Dr. Craigie's house, but the lights were turned off now except for one upstairs, and she could see

nothing happening. The house looked as solid and ordinary as usual. No one could guess that there was now a baby in there, not a sick child brought by its parents to Dr. Craigie's office, but a baby left all alone in the night on the doorstep.

Aristotle walked in sleepily from the pantry, wagging his tail. "Why didn't you bark, Aristotle?" Dorcas asked him. "You are some no-good watchdog." Aristotle grinned foolishly at her and went back to curl up on his cushion.

Dorcas got a glass of milk from the icebox and helped herself to a dish of rhubarb pudding. At least she would not be hungry while she waited.

The sound of the telephone ringing in the hall was unusually loud in the early-morning quiet. Dorcas lifted her head from the kitchen table. Somehow she had been half asleep, but with the ringing of the phone she was immediately wide-awake and remembering everything that had happened. She jumped up and ran to the hall.

"Hello?"

"Dorcas? This is Dr. Craigie. Sorry to call so early. Your father up yet?"

"I don't know. I don't think so. I'll go see."

Dorcas raced upstairs and knocked on her parents' bedroom door.

"Come in," her mother called. They were nearly dressed, Dorcas saw as she burst into the room.

"It's Dr. Craigie on the telephone, he wants to speak to you, Daddy. It must be about the baby." Her words tumbled out breathlessly.

"Baby? What baby?"

"The baby—I saw it—it was this morning—on his doorstep—"

"*Doorstep?* What on earth?" her mother exclaimed. "Reginald, do get on the telephone and find out what this is all about."

All three of them ran down the stairs, her father still with his clerical collar unbuttoned. Dorcas and her mother stood close by while Mr. Bennett spoke into the phone. But all they heard was, "Yes. . . . No. . . . Of course. . . . Yes indeed. . . ." And then, "We'll be right over."

Mr. Bennett hung up the receiver and looked at his wife with an odd expression. "Craigie wants us to come over immediately. It seems there *was* a baby left on his doorstep last night."

"I told you! Oh, Daddy, may I come, too? Please!" Dorcas pleaded. She could see right away it was no use.

"I'm sorry, Dorcas. This looks like a complicated situation. I don't know what it means yet. It's certainly nothing to get the whole town involved in."

"But I'm not the whole town!" Dorcas protested. "And I was the first one to know about it. I wasn't going to tell anybody but you—"

"Dorcas," her mother said firmly, "you will just have to be very patient until we see what this is all about. Don't say anything to anybody, even the boys. Just try to be helpful—you could get breakfast ready. We'll be back as soon as we can."

And, her father having buttoned his collar and her mother having pinned up her hair, they left, with Dorcas watching from the window seething with frustration and curiosity. It wasn't fair to have to stay home and make oatmeal porridge and set the table when something so exciting and mysterious was going on next door. And what was she going to say to Paul and Benjie if they got up and found their parents gone?

Fortunately, the boys did not come downstairs before

her parents, looking distinctly worried, came home. They sat down at the kitchen table and gratefully took the cups of coffee Dorcas served them.

"Thank you. That tastes good," said her father while Dorcas stood waiting, first on one foot and then on the other, scarcely able to contain her impatience.

"It's a strange story," her father began slowly. "We don't know much about it yet. The baby is a little girl, about ten days old. Who the father and mother are we have no idea. There was a note pinned on the blanket saying 'Please take care of this baby we can't.' That's all."

Dorcas's eyes widened. She was full of questions but kept silent while her mother spoke.

"Dr. Craigie has asked if we can take care of the baby—"

This was too much for Dorcas. "Oh, Mother!" she cried. "A baby sister! We can keep her, can't we?"

"Dorcas, this is just a temporary arrangement. Dr. Craigie is out much of the time, and his housekeeper, Mrs. Reilly, is eighty-two and can't be expected to be responsible for a new baby. We've offered to take her for a day or two until it's clear what's the best thing to do."

Dorcas's face fell, but before she could object, her mother said, "Let's go up to the attic and get the old cradle and some baby clothes. Reginald, you'd better hurry and finish breakfast or you'll be late for early service. Dorcas and I will go get the baby as soon as we have things ready here."

Dorcas flew about, helping to set up the cradle in the guest room next to her own bedroom, finding a box of diapers and nursing bottles last used by Benjie, and dusting off the beloved teddy bear she herself had put away only a year ago. Paul and Benjie, up now and popping with questions, could hardly believe what had happened.

Then Dorcas and her mother went next door, finding

Dr. Craigie and Mrs. Reilly in his office, where the basket stood on the examining table. Dorcas peeked in and saw the baby's round pink face. She was sleeping peacefully, her tiny hands curled like flower petals. She was quite perfect, Dorcas thought.

"Can you imagine such a shocking thing!" exclaimed Mrs. Reilly, shaking her head. "The poor little mite! Who could think of giving her up like that?"

"Now, Mrs. Reilly," Dr. Craigie scolded, "we don't know the reasons behind this yet. Don't be judging until you have the facts, and maybe not even then."

He picked up a paper from his desk. "The baby seems quite healthy. I've written down the formula—milk and rice water with a little sugar every four hours. It's very kind of you, Mrs. Bennett, to take this on. You may have a wakeful night or two before this is settled."

"Never mind, Doctor. We're glad to help out," Mrs. Bennett replied.

She picked up the baby, and Dorcas carried the basket across the lawn to the rectory. Paul and Benjie were waiting at the open front door.

"Gee whiskers, she's little!" cried Paul.

"Look at her fingernails!" said Benjie wonderingly.

"*Now* can I hold her myself?" demanded Dorcas.

"Yes, dear. Sit down and I'll put her right in your arms."

Dorcas sat in the living room in the big wing chair, holding the baby with extreme care. The baby opened her eyes for an instant. They were very dark blue and seemed to be seeing something far away. Her hair was only a few silky wisps of light reddish brown. Dorcas could see the soft place at the top of the baby's head where the beating of the pulse was visible.

"What do you suppose her name is?" Dorcas wondered.

"Nobody knows," her mother answered. "I wouldn't imagine she's been baptized."

"Could we give her a name?"

"Well, we could give her a temporary name. That would be better than just calling her Baby," her mother said. "I guess you have one already picked out?"

"Yes, I have," Dorcas responded. "It's Amy. You know, like Amy in *Little Women*."

"That sounds fine," her mother said approvingly. "But, Dorcas . . ." She hesitated. "Try not to get too fond of her."

"Oh, Mother, I love her already. *Can't* we keep her?"

"Please, Dorcas, don't ask for the impossible. Just be grateful we can help by taking care of her for a little while."

Dorcas tried not to let her mother's words spoil her happiness. When Amy had been tucked into the cradle, Dorcas sat beside her, rocking it gently and singing "Now the Day Is Over" and other quiet songs. Amy, fast asleep, did not hear them, but they made Dorcas feel better.

Nine

or the next few days, there was a constant stream of
helpful and curious visitors to the rectory. Everyone
wanted to see and talk about the Doorstep Baby. Miss
Henrietta came with her camera to take a photograph.
Miss Larrabee brought a tiny blanket she had sat up all
night crocheting. The ladies of the church brought stews
and cakes "because poor Mrs. Bennett is so busy taking
care of the baby she won't have time to cook." Julia came
in the mornings to help with the baby's bath and making
up the day's supply of bottles.

Dorcas could hardly wait to come home from school
every afternoon, and Maidie, of course, came with her.
All the other girls in the class begged to be allowed to visit
the baby, and Dorcas got permission from her mother to

let them come in groups of three, to stay for not more than fifteen minutes. Even Benjie's and Paul's friends were interested and poked their heads into the baby's bedroom at unexpected moments. Nothing so exciting had happened in quiet little Gordontown since the tiger's escape from the circus train in 1926.

Dorcas loved giving Amy her bottle and changing her diapers. She wouldn't have minded getting up in the middle of the night to feed the baby, but Mrs. Bennett refused to permit that. "You must get your proper sleep, Dorcas. I'll set the alarm for the two-o'clock feeding, and if you hear it, or hear the baby cry, I want you to just turn over and go back to sleep. I'll take care of it."

Dorcas saw that both her mother and her father were very tired in the mornings and knew that their night's rest had been interrupted several times. She wished she could stay and take care of Amy during the day, but of course she was expected to go to school just as if nothing disturbing and wonderful had happened at home.

Dorcas was home on Monday afternoon when the town constable came around and asked all sorts of questions. Mr. and Mrs. Bennett could tell him very little. "We know only what Dr. Craigie told us about finding her," explained Mr. Bennett. "Just that he heard the crying at about four-thirty Sunday morning, opened his front door, and found the basket with the baby in it on the doorstep. There was the note asking him to care for it, nothing more."

"There were no markings on the baby's clothing or blankets," Mrs. Bennett added.

"And you have no suspicions as to the parentage of this infant?" inquired the constable, with pencil poised over the notebook where he was carefully writing down everything that was said.

Dorcas saw her father and mother exchange a glance that suddenly gave her the idea that they knew more than they were telling.

"We have no information on that, Officer," Mr. Bennett said quietly.

"You and Dr. Craigie are custodians of this infant?" asked the constable.

"There is nothing official about it," Mr. Bennett replied. "We are simply caring for the baby until we can find out what the situation is."

Frowning, the constable wrote this down slowly, then asked, "Are you making inquiries?"

"Yes, of course, with Dr. Craigie we are asking anyone who might have any information to let us know," Mr. Bennett told him. "Privacy would be assured to any informant, it is understood."

"And we know that *you* are making a very thorough investigation," Mrs. Bennett said, smiling at the constable, who looked pleased and embarrassed.

The constable left not much wiser than when he'd arrived, though he did take a look at Amy, who returned his stare unblinkingly. She was pronounced "a pretty little thing" by the constable, who departed, stuffing his notebook in his vest pocket and shaking his head.

There were long conversations going on from time to time behind the closed doors of Dorcas's father's study. Sometimes it was her father with Dr. Craigie, or one of the vestrymen of the church. Sometimes it was just her parents talking in low tones. Dorcas knew better than to try to listen at the door, but she was very uneasy about these solemn conferences, for she was sure they had to do with what would happen to Amy. She wanted with all her heart to keep this baby as the little sister she had wished for so long. She couldn't see any reason why that wouldn't be the best thing for everybody concerned.

One morning when their mother had not come down to supervise their breakfast, Dorcas talked about it to Paul.

"Don't you think we ought to keep Amy?" she asked directly as she poured milk on her oatmeal.

Paul answered without hesitation. " 'Course. Why not?"

"I don't know why not. Mother and Daddy keep saying it's only temporary, we mustn't expect to have her forever. But she's no trouble at all, and if there are two boys in the family there ought to be two girls."

Dorcas was afraid Paul would make a silly remark about that, but he only looked at her with his bright gray eyes and said seriously, "That's right. Two and two make four. That's a good number."

"Paul, why don't you tell them? It can't be just me arguing all the time."

Paul drank the last of his milk with the loud gurgling sound forbidden by his mother. "Sure. I'll tell 'em. I'll get Benjie too. He likes Amy even if she is too little to play with. I told him she'd grow up."

"Oh, thank you, Paul!" Dorcas was relieved and grateful that Paul had not needed any persuasion. Sometimes a brother could be surprisingly understanding.

School let out early Friday afternoon, and Dorcas went right home, without Maidie, who had to go to Miss Larrabee's for a piano lesson. The house was quiet when she entered, her mother not in the kitchen, her father's study empty. Dorcas ran upstairs and found Julia sitting in the rocking chair beside the cradle, holding Amy, who was fast asleep.

"Julia! You're here! How is Amy? Where are Mother and Daddy?"

"Amy's just fine, just finished her bottle. You can see

she's already fatter than she was five days ago. Just look at her face—why she's getting a double chin!" Julia laughed.

Dorcas leaned over to inspect Amy's placid little face and agreed that, yes, she was indeed fatter, and her cheeks were rosier than they'd been that Sunday morning only a few days ago.

"Isn't it funny, Julia," Dorcas said. "Just last week we didn't know Amy was in the world. Now that's all we think about. I can't imagine her *not* being."

"I know," Julia answered, rocking softly. "That's what happens with babies. That's what happened with you when you were born."

"I guess it did," Dorcas replied, thinking for the first time how her own coming had changed her parents' life.

"Your mother and father went off after lunch with Dr. Craigie in his automobile," Julia told Dorcas. "They should be back within the hour, I'd think."

Dorcas wanted to hold Amy, but Julia looked so contented that she didn't suggest it. Instead she fetched her drawing tablet and drew a sketch of Julia and the baby. The hard part was the bottom of the rocking chair; no matter how she tried, Dorcas's picture made the rockers look like runners on a sled.

She was working away at her drawing when she heard her parents come in, and she didn't run to greet them. She heard voices and realized that Dr. Craigie had come in with them, and perhaps someone else. When her mother appeared at the bedroom door ten minutes later, she was carrying a tray of glasses of iced tea and a plate of ginger snaps.

"Just the thing!" cried Julia, laying Amy tenderly in the cradle. Dorcas put down her sketch pad and joined her mother and Julia in a little tea party.

Afterward, Dorcas took the tray down to the kitchen. There were voices to be heard coming from behind her father's closed study door, and when she went back upstairs she found the door to Amy's bedroom shut and her mother and Julia talking earnestly, their words too soft to be made out.

Dorcas was cross. So much talking going on, everything secret. Why couldn't she know what was going on? She stomped noisily down the stairs and went out to sit on the porch swing, pushing angrily back and forth, feeling sorry for herself and annoyed with everyone else.

When the front door opened, Dr. Craigie came out with another man, a shabby stooped figure in overalls who somehow seemed familiar. It was Mr. Baxter, Grover's father. She had seen him that Easter Day on the walk with her father when they'd stopped at the Baxter farm. She had a sudden sharp memory of the house and the farmyard, the rusty farm machinery and the battered old automobile by the sagging front porch. Whatever was Mr. Baxter doing here? Dorcas kept perfectly quiet, and Dr. Craigie and Mr. Baxter did not notice her as they went down the steps and got into Dr. Craigie's car at the curb.

Dorcas sat in the swing for some minutes, thinking. She had been taught not to ask too many questions about the people who came and went in consultations with her father. She realized that an important part of his job was to advise and comfort people, and it would not do for his daughter to be snoopy and talk about them. But now there was a problem right in their own house, and if Dorcas was part of the family she ought not to be left out of everything. There were too many mysteries.

The more she thought about it, the more Dorcas felt outraged and hurt. She wanted to storm at her parents and demand that she be told what was happening. But when she imagined confronting them with her angry accusations, she could also imagine their telling her once more that she must control her temper. Somehow she would have to make herself be calm and reasonable and then maybe they would stop treating her like a little child who didn't need to be told what was going on.

Dorcas jumped out of the swing and went into the house, her back straight and her mouth in a determined line.

Ten

The door to Mr. Bennett's study was open and he was sitting at his desk writing something on a sheet of yellow paper. Dorcas stood silently, hoping her father would look up and see her. When he did, he smiled. "Come in, dear. I haven't seen much of you lately. We've all been so preoccupied with little Amy."

Dorcas perched next to the desk in the comfortable old armchair where so many people had sat to tell Mr. Bennett their troubles. She felt quite in control of her temper, and it was a good strong feeling. But she did not know quite how to begin asking all the questions that whirled in her brain. At last she blurted out, "What is happening, Daddy? Where did Amy come from and what's going to happen to her and why can't we keep her?"

Her father turned around in his swivel chair and made his fingers into a steeple. He looked thoughtfully out the window for a moment and then at Dorcas.

"I believe you deserve to know what we've found out, my child. I'm sure we can trust you not to talk about it indiscreetly. It's a very sad business, but we can hope some good is coming from it." He paused and drummed his fingers lightly on the desk.

"You remember our Easter walk?" Dorcas nodded her head vigorously. "You saw the Baxter farm then and perhaps understood that Mr. Baxter was having a very difficult time, with a sick wife and not enough income from his farm to support his family. There are five little boys, you know."

"Yes, I know. Grover is in my grade, remember? But he hasn't been coming to school for a long time, not since the play when he wasn't there to be Telemachus."

"Yes, I recall that dramatic crisis," her father said, with a faint smile. "Well, Grover was not there, hasn't been back, because of a family tragedy. What happened was this. Mr. Baxter heard from his brother about a job at a dairy farm in Maxwell County, some hundred miles from here. So he took all his family—his wife and the five boys—and their belongings. Loaded them all into that old flivver and set off."

"How could they all get in that car?" Dorcas asked in dismay. "It didn't look as if it would run anyway."

"No, it didn't, but somehow Mr. Baxter fixed it up with wires, cranked the engine, and got it going. I'm sure it was a rough journey, with the engine breaking down often. And Mrs. Baxter was expecting a baby."

Dorcas tried to imagine it, and shuddered.

"They had just arrived at the dairy farm, and Mr. Baxter was told he could have the job and a little house for

78

the family, when Mrs. Baxter had the baby."

"It was Amy?" cried Dorcas.

"Yes, it was Amy. Apparently it was a difficult birth, and Mrs. Baxter had a heart condition. When Amy was three days old, Mrs. Baxter died."

Dorcas swallowed hard. The thought of a baby without a mother was too sad to contemplate.

"So what did they do—Mr. Baxter and Grover and his brothers?"

"They tried to take care of the baby themselves. But of course Mr. Baxter had to be at work all day, and the boys really didn't know how to tend to a newborn. Poor Mr. Baxter was desperate. He didn't have any relatives who could help. He thought of Dr. Craigie, who had always been kind to them when they lived here. So one day he just put the baby in the car and drove back to Gordontown and left her on the doorstep for Dr. Craigie to find."

"Oh, he must have felt terrible when he had to leave her!" Dorcas felt hot tears stinging in her eyes.

"Of course he did, but he couldn't think of anything else to do. He knew Dr. Craigie would care for the baby somehow. He just drove back to his boys and trusted he'd done the best for her."

"But he could have come and *asked* Dr. Craigie. He could have come and asked *us!*"

"Yes, he should have done that, but you know how when people are in terrible trouble sometimes they can't think straight."

Dorcas nodded her head. Indeed she knew. She remembered how when she'd been angry or afraid she'd done some things she'd rather not think about.

"How did you find that the baby belonged to the Baxters?"

"Dr. Craigie recalled that Mrs. Baxter was expecting,

79

though she hadn't been in to see him for some time. And we knew the family was having hard times. So we went to the farm, found them gone, and asked the neighbors. They didn't know much about it, but they told us they thought the Baxters had gone to Maxwell County. We got in touch with the police there and found that Mrs. Baxter had died. Dr. Craigie went there to see Mr. Baxter and brought him back here to talk things over."

"Is he going to take Amy away now?" Dorcas asked in alarm.

"He would like to have her, naturally, but he's simply not in a position to keep her."

Just then Dorcas heard her mother saying goodbye to Julia at the front door. Mrs. Bennett came into the study and sat down beside Dorcas.

"Then shouldn't we keep Amy? Couldn't we?" Dorcas pleaded, looking first at her father and then at her mother. "We have a room for her and she's getting nice and fat with all that good milk and I'm sure she knows me already! Oh, please!" Dorcas saw her mother shaking her head, and her heart sank. "Why not? Why not?"

"Dorcas, we understand how you feel," her father said kindly. "We love Amy, too. But there are a number of reasons why we can't keep her."

"We already have our family, dear," said her mother. "And your father and I are not as young as we were." This was something Dorcas had not considered. She did not think of her father as old, but she knew he had been fifty-two on his last birthday; her mother was nine years younger.

"But *I* can take care of her!" Dorcas exclaimed.

"When you are home from school, you are a great help," her mother said. "But you aren't here most of the day. Amy sleeps a lot now, but soon she'll need much more attention, and when she starts walking she'll have to be watched every moment. It is a very great responsibility, having a child, and it goes on for many years."

"Oh, dear, then what will happen? Will Amy have to go to an orphan asylum?" At this thought, Dorcas burst into tears.

"Now, Dorcas, don't be upset. You know if there were no other answer, we would keep Amy," her father told her. "We'd never let her go to an orphanage."

"Then what *is* going to happen to her?" Dorcas choked out.

"Something wonderful," said her mother. "Just think for a moment. Whom do we know who hasn't any children, some people who want a baby very much and would make splendid parents?"

Dorcas shook her head in confusion. Then her face lit up. When she spoke, it was almost in a shout:

"Julia and Albert!"

"Yes," Mrs. Bennett said. "Julia and Albert. There will be some legal matters to take care of, but Mr. Baxter has agreed. As soon as it can be managed, Julia and Albert are going to adopt Amy."

Dorcas felt too many conflicting emotions tumbling about in her stomach and chest. Her worry and disappointment were all mixed up with relief and gratitude.

"If I can't have a baby sister, the next best thing is for Julia and Albert to have Amy," she pronounced, rubbing away the last tear. '

"Not the next best, *the* best thing," her father said. "Best for everyone, particularly Amy."

"I'm going to see Julia and Albert right now!" Dorcas cried, hurrying out the door before anyone could point out that the Abbots might like a little time to themselves to get used to the idea of being parents.

Eleven

Walking down Liberty Street, Dorcas tried to sort out her feelings. She had been so eager to keep Amy in her own family that she hadn't seen the obvious solution. Of course Julia and Albert ought to have Amy. They were the ones who needed and wanted her most. And if Dorcas couldn't have Amy at home, she would be only four blocks away. She could see her nearly every day.

When she walked by the park, Dorcas almost didn't notice the man sitting on a bench near the Civil War monument. She kept on walking, then slowed her steps. Looking back, she saw that the man was Mr. Baxter. His head was bowed, his hands clenched on his knees. He looked so sorrowful that Dorcas's heart ached. Before she could think twice, she turned around and went into the park.

Mr. Baxter glanced up and saw her standing beside him. He didn't seem to recognize her.

Dorcas stood awkwardly, unable to think of what to say. At last she gulped out, "I'm Dorcas Bennett. You know—we've been keeping Amy . . . the baby—your baby . . ."

Mr. Baxter looked directly at her. "Yes. Yes. I see who you are now." He swallowed hard. "Your family's been real good." His mouth trembled, and he put up his fist to hide it.

Dorcas hastened to speak. "We loved taking care of Amy. She's a beautiful baby. We just love her . . ."

A look of such pain crossed his lined and tired face that Dorcas could not endure it. She knelt down beside the bench and put out her hand, almost touching his workworn one.

"Julia and Albert love her, too, and they'll take such good care of her—you don't have to worry a bit."

"I ain't worried. I believe they will take good care." He paused and coughed. "Only thing, I wish it was Laura-belle. My wife. Always wanted a little girl. But with her gone, I can't do it. Can't bring up the child right. Grover and the boys tried to help me. But we can't do it. She needs a mother."

Dorcas bit her lip. She had been thinking so much about her own family and Amy and now Julia and Albert that she hadn't thought enough about what giving up the baby meant to the Baxters. Her father had said it was the best solution for everybody, but what about Mr. Baxter? It was the worst grief she had ever seen.

"Mr. Baxter—I'm so sorry. Sorry about your wife, I

83

mean, and you, and Grover and the rest of your boys. I think it's very brave of you to let Amy go to Julia and Albert. They've wanted a baby for a long time. I even prayed for a miracle so Julia could have one. I guess getting Amy is a kind of miracle—for them, I mean. But not for you, exactly, is it?" Her voice trailed off. She could think of no more comforting words.

Mr. Baxter shook his head and sat in silent misery.

Dorcas looked desperately out to the street. If only her father would come by this minute! He would know what to say. But there was no one, no one at all.

Her eyes fell on the statue of the Civil War soldier. The slanting late-afternoon sunlight touched the soldier's up-lifted head and the inscription on the pedestal:

In grateful memory of the heroes of Gordontown, who sacrificed for the cause of the Union.

Suddenly, she knew what to say.

"Mr. Baxter," she began earnestly, hoping it would come out right. "It's like those people on the monument. Making a sacrifice for the cause. That's what you're doing."

Mr. Baxter, bewildered, looked where Dorcas was pointing.

"See, those names on the monument. The men who went off to the Civil War. You aren't going off like a soldier, but you're making a sacrifice for a cause. That's what a hero does. You're doing it for Amy. You're a hero, Mr. Baxter."

Mr. Baxter blinked his eyes and sat wordlessly looking at the memorial. At last he spoke in a raspy voice.

"Nobody'd call me a hero. But I thank you, young lady, for your kindly thought."

Dorcas stood up and brushed the grass off her knees.

"I'm going to the Abbots' house right now. Why don't you come, too? You could see where they live—where Amy's going to live, how nice it is. I'm sure they'll want you to come and visit her whenever you come back."

Mr. Baxter looked distressed. "Couldn't do that, could I?"

"Of course you could. Amy will just have two families, that's all. Come on." Dorcas took Mr. Baxter's hand, and he rose and went limping down the street with her as if he were walking in his sleep.

Julia was standing at the gate. She looked at both of them with a troubled glance. Then her face cleared and she opened the gate to welcome them. "Mr. Baxter—Dorcas—come in, come in."

Mr. Baxter held back, but Julia took him gently by the elbow and led him through the gate.

"I'm so glad you've come to see where Amy will be living," Julia told him warmly. "We want you to come whenever you can, and Amy's brothers too."

Mr. Baxter mumbled something that sounded like "Thank you."

"And, Mr. Baxter, I want to ask you something," Julia went on. "It's about the baby's name. You know we've been calling her Amy—it was Dorcas's choice—and we'd like to keep on calling her that because it's a lovely name. It means beloved, you know, and that she certainly is. But we'd like to give her a second name, and we think it should be her mother's. Would you approve of that?"

Mr. Baxter's face lightened for the first time. "Well, now, yes, ma'am, I surely would like that."

"What was Mrs. Baxter's name?"

Mr. Baxter spoke it softly: "Laurabelle. Her name was Laurabelle."

"Oh, that's so pretty!" Julia cried. "She'll be Amy Laurabelle, then. What do you think, Dorcas? Doesn't that sound right?"

"Yes, it does," Dorcas answered, following them into the house. "Amy Laurabelle. It's a long name for such a little baby, maybe, but it does sound just right."

Twelve

I t was a brisk late-October day, the afternoon sunbeams touching the trees along Liberty Street with a brilliant golden light. Dorcas skipped along the sidewalk, swinging her school bag even though it was heavy with books. Miss McLain, the sixth-grade teacher, believed in assigning lots of homework. She was strict, but Dorcas liked the way she talked to her pupils as if she thought they were pretty mature and ought not to be treated like first-graders.

There were days when Dorcas felt really grown-up, now that she had gotten two inches taller during the summer and was on her way to her twelfth birthday. It had been a lovely summer, starting with a June confirmation service in which Dorcas became a full member of the church, then trips to the lake for swims and picnics, working on an illustrated storybook with Maidie, and, best of all, spending an hour or so every day helping to care for Amy. Julia had let Dorcas change Amy's clothes, give her a bath, feed her, and take her for outings in the pram. It was generous of Julia, Dorcas realized, for she herself took such pleasure in caring for Amy that she might not have been willing to share so much.

It was in August, after all the legal questions had been taken care of and Amy was officially adopted, that Julia had said to Dorcas, "We've been thinking about having Amy christened soon. Your father has been talking to us about it. You know a baby has to have three godparents, and we're going to ask my brother and Albert's sister. How would *you* like to be a godmother?"

Dorcas was overwhelmed. It was most unusual for anyone so young to be considered as a godparent, but her father agreed that she was responsible enough to accept. It had been a beautiful christening, with Amy in a long white dress made by Mrs. Bennett. Dorcas too had a new dress, not a childish smocked one but a green linen with a lace collar and a belt instead of a sash. The church had been full—Miss Larrabee, Miss Henrietta Bishop and Miss Endicott sitting together in the pew behind Mrs. Bennett and Paul and Benjie. Dr. Craigie had been there, too, looking very pleased about everything.

Dorcas stood at the baptismal font with Julia's brother and Albert's sister, while Amy was held by her mother, and Albert beamed beside her. When her father spoke the traditional phrases of the service, Dorcas felt very solemn. The words sounded clearly in the quiet church: "Name this child." Dorcas and the other two godparents answered in unison: "Amy Laurabelle." Dorcas felt a warm glow in her chest to think that she had been the one to choose Amy's first name and that Julia and Albert had not wanted to change it. And having her own mother's name would mean a great deal to Amy when she grew up, Julia had pointed out.

It was probably too late this afternoon to take Amy for a stroll. Dorcas had stayed after school for choral practice. The sixth grade was going to join with the junior-high-school singers in a Thanksgiving concert. Maidie and Richard were in the chorus, too, all of them learning about part-singing. Dorcas ran up the path to the Abbots' house, humming the tune to "Bringing in the Sheaves."

"Come in!" Julia called. "I've just brought Amy in from her walk. Look how rosy she is from all that October air!"

Dorcas picked up the baby, who was still wearing the little pink bonnet Miss Larrabee had knitted for her. "Oh, you darling!" Dorcas exclaimed, and Amy gurgled and smiled in response.

"She's sitting up all the time now," Julia said proudly. "And her tooth is almost through. I took her to see Dr. Craigie this morning and he says she's in perfect health."

"You're just perfect, that's all!" Dorcas told Amy, who grinned and reached up to give Dorcas's braid a surprisingly hard pull.

"Now, Dorcas, you entertain Amy while I get her a cracker and some refreshments for you and me. Make yourself comfortable. You and I are going to have a good long talk."

Dorcas fitted herself into the sofa cushions with Amy on her lap, while the fading sunlight slanted across the red carpet. The house was warm and smelled faintly of the bread Julia had baked that morning. From the kitchen came the clinking sounds of cups and saucers being set out on a tray.

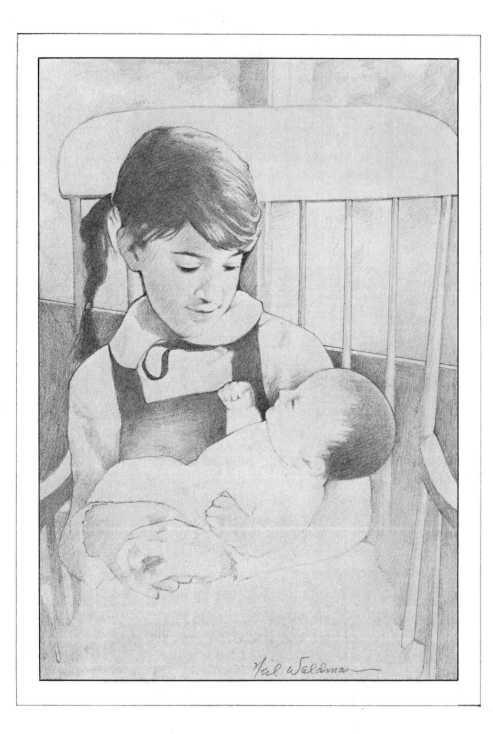

"Amy," Dorcas said into the baby's ear, "someday you will be drinking out of those old hand-painted teacups your great-grandma made."

Amy gave a hiccup, and then laughed aloud at her own funny noise.

It was almost dark, but Dorcas hardly noticed where she put her feet as she dashed homeward. She was out of breath when she arrived at the front door. Flinging off her coat, she rushed into the kitchen. Her mother was at the stove peering into a bubbling pot of rice. Her father sat at the kitchen table reading aloud from the newspaper about next month's presidential election.

"That's very interesting, what Mr. Roosevelt says he plans to do if he's elected, don't you think, dear?" Mrs. Bennett said absently, taking the pot to the sink to drain it.

"Mother! Daddy! Listen!" Dorcas gasped. "I have the most important news—you will not believe it—"

"More important than who's to be President?" inquired Mr. Bennett with a smile.

"Yes, oh, yes! Just listen—you won't believe it!" Dorcas's eyes were shining, and her breath still came in noisy heaves.

"Whatever is it, dear?" Mrs. Bennett asked, really paying attention at last.

"Julia just told me. It's the biggest surprise in the world. Julia—Julia—she's going to have a baby!"

"Going to—what do you mean? She *has* a baby." Mrs. Bennett looked altogether puzzled.

"Yes, of course, they have Amy. She's their first baby. And now—now—Julia's going to have another one herself!"

"Well, well, well," said Mr. Bennett, taking off his spectacles and shaking his head in astonishment.

"That *is* a surprise," Mrs. Bennett declared, her face lit with pleasure. "I've heard of this happening sometimes after a couple adopts a baby. My, Julia and Albert must be very happy."

"They're so happy they can hardly stand it!" Dorcas laughed. "They waited so long, and then at last they got Amy, and now there will be a little sister for her. Or maybe a brother. Julia and Albert always wanted lots of children."

Mrs. Bennett stood, the pot of rice forgotten, a smile of amazement still curving her lips. "God works in mysterious ways His wonders to perform," she said softly.

Mr. Bennett took Dorcas's hand and squeezed it affectionately. "Do you remember talking about praying for a miracle for someone else?" he asked.

"Yes, Daddy. It was a miracle for Julia I was praying for, and it did happen, she got Amy. I didn't pray anymore after that—Amy was the answer. Even if it wasn't exactly the way I'd imagined. And now there are *two* miracles!"

She stopped short, remembering what else her father had said. Slowly she spoke again.

"Sometimes, we don't get what we asked for. Sometimes we get something different, and better. And sometimes, when we don't expect it, when we haven't even asked for it, a miracle is *given!*"

About the author

Lee Pennock Huntington has lived and worked in many parts of the world. She taught in Bogotá, Colombia, served on the Quaker Relief team in North Africa and was a member of the Quaker representation at the United Nations in New York. She is the author of several children's books, including *Simple Shelters* and *Americans At Home.* She presently reviews books for the Rutland, Vermont *Sunday Herald, Horticulture Magazine* and the Book-of-the-Month Club.

Mrs. Huntington is the mother of three children. She lives with her husband, an architect, in Rochester, Vermont.